This book belongs to ·······························

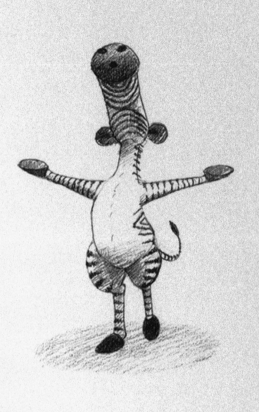

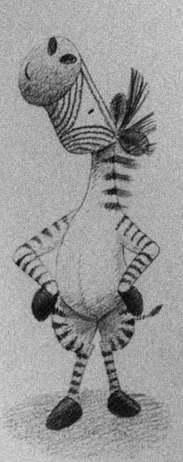

To John Travolta

D.B.

For my nephew, Alexander,
a definite future groover!

R.J.

EGMONT
We bring stories to life

First published in Great Britain 2008
by Egmont UK Limited
239 Kensington High Street
London W8 6SA

Text copyright © David Bedford 2008
Illustrations copyright © Russell Julian 2008

The moral rights of the author and illustrator have been asserted

ISBN 978 14052 2804 6 (Hardback)
ISBN 978 14052 2805 3 (Paperback)

3 5 7 9 10 8 6 4 2

A CIP catalogue record for this title is available from the British Library

Printed and bound in Italy

It's a **George Thing!**

David Bedford   Russell Julian

EGMONT

George had two best friends,

Peachy and **Moon**.

Every morning, George went to
Peachy's house to play Big Ball.

Playing Big Ball was a **Peachy Thing**.
It was the thing Peachy liked best.

George wasn't very good at it.

Every afternoon, George went to
Moon's house to play Rocks.

Playing Rocks was a **Moon Thing**.
It was the thing Moon liked best.

George didn't understand it.

One day, when George was walking home from Moon's house,
he heard a new sound coming from Priscilla's River Boat.

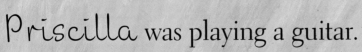 was playing a guitar.
                    And when she began singing . . .

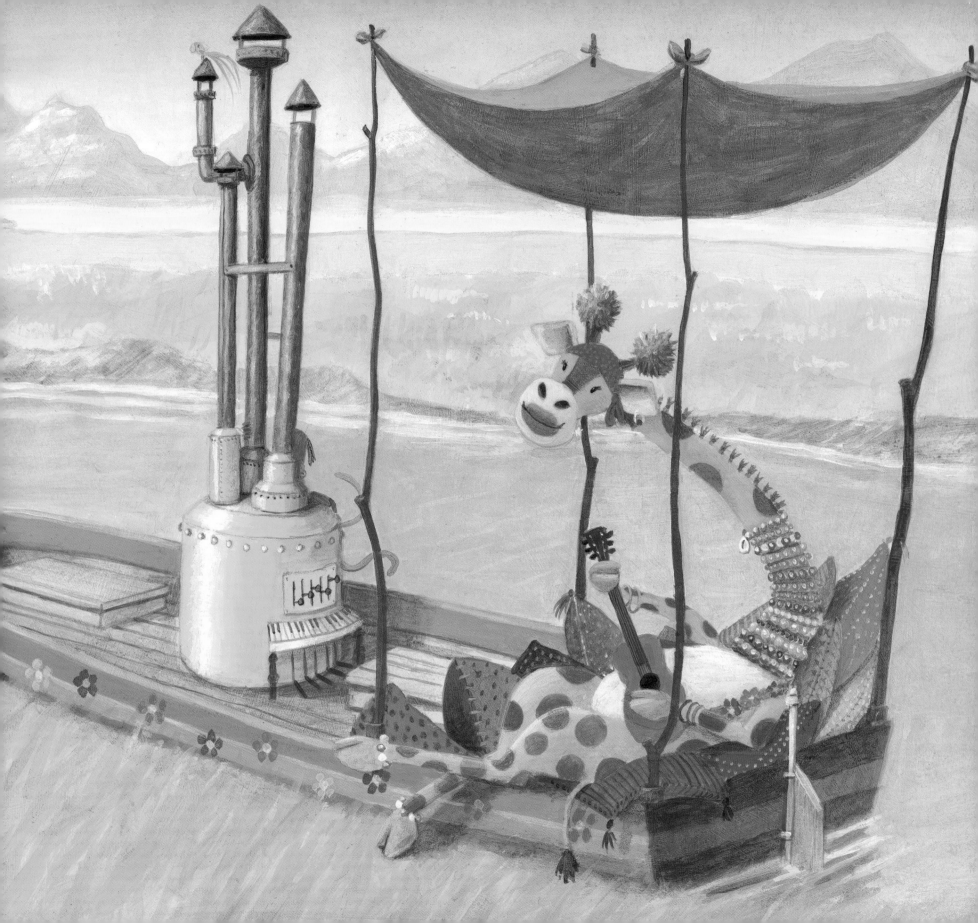

. . . **George** did this!

"You're a really
good dancer, George,"
said Priscilla. "I'm
putting you in my Show tonight.
It's at 7 o'clock.
Don't be late!"

George had to hurry
to get ready . . .

. . . but it took ages
to find something
to wear.

Then he checked the time.

"I'm late!"
yelled George.

Geooooorrrge!

On his way to the Show,
George saw Peachy and Moon looking for him,
so he hid where they would never look.

He didn't think his friends would understand.

When George finally arrived at
the Show, he had a surprise.
It looked like the whole jungle was there!

George felt very nervous.
But when Priscilla began to sing . . .

. . . George did this!

And this!

And this!

And this!

George was having
so much fun!

But then . . .

. . . George froze.

      Everyone was staring at him.

He had never felt so alone.

Priscilla was still singing, but George couldn't move.

Then suddenly there was someone beside him.
And another someone.

It was **Peachy**   and **Moon**!

"I'm not very good at this," puffed Peachy.
"I don't understand it!" huffed Moon. "I don't even know what it is."

George grinned. "It's a **George Thing!**" he said
and he showed his friends how to do it.

From then on,
George still went
to Peachy's house
    to do **Peachy Things**.

And he still went
to Moon's house
    to do **Moon Things**.

But sometimes they all got together to do . . .

. . . a George Thing!

Start with a **scratch**

Push your chest up **high**

Tickle
your chin

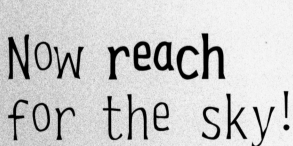

Now **reach**
for the sky!

Take a **silly walk**

Do your own things!

Say 'bye-bye'

Now spread your **wings!**